WHEN IT RAINS

THE SHORT STORY PREQUELS TO THE ANGUS
MURDERS MYSTERIES SERIES

ALLAN L MANN

NOIR CAFÉ PRESS

First paperback edition August 2019

Cover design by Nick Castle

Author photograph by Allan L Mann

Library of Congress Control Number: 2019909756

ISBN 978-1-7329227-2-3 (paperback)

ISBN 978-1-7329227-3-0 (ebook)

Published by: Noir Café Press, LLC

www.NoirCafePress.com

To Christy, who puts up with all of my projects.

To Mum and Dad, who still worry about me.
I like that.

INTRODUCTION

The two short stories contained in WHEN IT RAINS helped me craft the character of Tom Guthrie for a trilogy in THE ANGUS MURDERS MYSTERIES series.

I felt I needed to know him a little before I embarked on the trilogy—to find out what he was going to be like, how he thought, the decisions he would make.

What I discovered was the way he quickly developed his personality. He began thinking and doing things I might do in some situations and ended up doing his own thing, leaving me wondering why he did this or that. There were times I was writing and knew such and such was going to happen—then it didn't, it went in a completely different direction.

This is the creative process.

I hope you enjoy your time with Guthrie and learn as much as I did about him.

— Allan L Mann

Georgetown, KY, July 2019

WRUNG OUT

ONE

It was moonless and cold, the damp air penetrating Jock Bishop's jacket making it feel colder than it was, so he turned up the collar, hunched his shoulders, and shoved his hands as deep into his pockets as possible.

That's when he felt it.

It was a sickening blow to the back of his head. His legs immediately stopped working and he fell to his knees then flat onto the pavement, face first. With his hands in his pockets he couldn't cushion his fall even if he wanted to. His face hit the wet surface hard enough that his right cheek bone cracked. He managed to free one hand and tried to push himself up.

Then the kicks came. Some to his chest and stomach, others to his back.

Slowly, the world faded. He felt like he was falling asleep in fast forward.

The beating continued as Jock Bishop slipped into unconsciousness. He would die later that morning.

TWO

Tom Guthrie pinned the man against the wall of the public toilets, pushing his face into the cold tile of the wall. He kneed him in the back of his right leg, forcing him to collapse slightly, his hands now caught between his beer belly and the urinal.

"What's wrong, Franky-boy? Little shy or are you finished?

"Shite!"

"Oh really, Franky? You do know you're doing it all wrong? Perhaps I can help."

Detective Sergeant Tom Guthrie grabbed the back of the man's shirt collar in one hand and his belt in the other, spun him around and slammed him into a cubicle door which, in turn, crashed off the side wall. Guthrie threw the short, thirty something Glaswegian against the grubby toilet.

"Shite!" was all Franky could manage again as he struggled to extricate himself from between the toilet bowl and the wall of the cubicle where he had landed. Little bits of toilet tissue were sticking to one leg of his designer jeans, one knee of which was now a little wet. Probably not with water. Once on his feet he quickly rearranged himself and zipped his fly.

"Franky-boy—sit down." Guthrie indicated the white plastic seat, covered with stains of uncertain origin.

"Aw, c'mon, Mister Guthrie," Franky protested. "Gonnie no make me sit on that in ma gid jeans, eh?"

"Aye, I am. Sit." Franky mumbled another protest but gingerly perched himself on the front lip of the public commode.

"Now, Franky. Tell me what you know about what happened to Jock Bishop."

"I told you, Mister Guthrie, I don't know onythin'"

"Oh, come off it, Franky." Guthrie kicked the door of the neighboring cubicle to punctuate his frustration. "You and I both know that's not quite kosher, eh?"

"Look, I tol' you aw'hing back at the nick and I'm no about tae tell you awny'hing diff'rent, 'cos a've nuh'ing tae add."

Guthrie stared at Franky and let the silence linger. Franky started to pick the bits of toilet tissue off his jeans, flicking them back onto the wet floor.

"Franky, let me just clear the air here."

"No much chance o' that in here, eh?"

Guthrie raised an eyebrow and actually admired the fact Franky could still crack a funny line having just been thrown around a public toilet. Being brought up in the harder parts of Glasgow would do that to you. "Point taken. Still, I know you had nothing to do with Jock's death, but I know you know more than you're letting on. In fact, you know who did kill him and I'm willing to bet you actually want to tell me because you're fed up with me and my colleagues harassing you every other day for something you had no part in. Am I right?"

This time it was Franky who let the silence fill the damp air. He pulled the remaining three sheets of toilet tissue from the roll secured to the cubicle wall and started to dab his wet knee.

Guthrie leaned forward, his hands holding on to each side of the door frame.

"Well? Am I right?"

Franky looked up and quietly said, "Aye."

THREE

The formal interview of Francis "Franky" Davidson, back at Divisional Headquarters of Tayside Police on West Bell Street, Dundee, was conducted in a more structured manner than the unofficial, "conversation" that took place in the gents' lavatory by the Wellgate shopping center a couple of hours earlier. Franky related to Guthrie and Detective Inspector Ian Buchanan what he knew about the death of Jock Bishop, including names of those responsible, timing, places.

Guthrie leaned one shoulder against the wall opposite the door of the interview room as Buchanan stepped into the hallway. He nodded his head towards the room, "Result."

Closing the door behind him Buchanan paused only long enough to glare at Guthrie before striding down the hall to the CID room. Guthrie sighed and looked down at the well-worn gray carpet.

Pushing himself upright he shoved his hands into his pockets and followed after Buchanan.

He knew what was coming.

FOUR

When Guthrie opened the door of the CID room, Buchanan was already sitting at his desk. DI Buchanan had spent the past five years as a Detective Sergeant and had been newly promoted prior to a move out of CID to take over as the senior officer running the Arbroath station. It was widely rumored that he would steadily climb the promotion ladder and end up going down the administrative track and on to bigger and better things. Over the past two years he had been working alongside Guthrie.

To say they were like oil and water would be like saying Rangers and Celtic football fans were partisan.

Guthrie didn't much care for the "touchy-feely" way of policing. He would put himself firmly in the camp of old school. He didn't like the work that was being done to implement a plan to create a Tayside Police presence on social media. It wasn't that he didn't understand it—sure, he wasn't the least bit interested in websites like Facebook and the rest—it was more a belief that if you wanted to effectively police a community, a city, you had to physically see and be seen. This applied to those who you were trying to protect from muggings, burglaries and worse, but also to those who were doing the mugging, burglaries and worse.

If you wanted to make sure the shops down the high street were secure, you walked your beat and shook hands with the door handles. If you wanted to know who was up to no good, you talked with friends and associates. You hung out in the pubs, you talked to people in the community. You did old-fashioned coppering.

It was his opinion that the Force—even the word was frowned upon now as too aggressive—was becoming soft. Yes, there was a place for a softer side to being a police officer, but there was certainly a time and a place for shoving someone's face into the cold, condensation covered tile of a public restroom.

Buchanan was a product of modern policing. He was budget conscious and placed more importance in polished shoes and perfect paperwork than Guthrie thought was healthy. His desk looked like an advert for Ikea—only the essentials won the right to take their place on the hallowed space that was Buchanan's desk. There was a flat screen monitor, keyboard and mouse in prime position in the middle of the highly polished wood laminate surface. A black wire in-tray occupied the left side, perfectly placed exactly at the midpoint of the desk's depth. The right side included a small notepad and a Tulliallen Police College coffee mug containing a couple of mechanical pencils and pens.

The man himself was an athletic six foot, one hundred and eighty pounds. His black hair was cut short and always trimmed. His white shirt and black trousers were highly pressed, and Guthrie wouldn't want to know how much he spent on designer ties.

Guthrie was no slouch, but his priorities were a little different. Since hitting forty his metabolism had slowed down along with enthusiasm for working out. His mountain bike spent more and more time inside than on the many trails around the country and his weight had slowly topped two hundred. Work was his life. To the detriment of his relationship with his wife, Jean.

She had quietly put up with weeks on end of Guthrie working twelve to fifteen hours a day during investigations. Their social life, her social life, was nonexistent. She had said she blamed herself for that. It was, however, an affair with a friend that had sealed the fate of the marriage.

Guthrie had suspected for some time and started to put the clues together after going to a play both Jean and "the other man"—he vowed never to use his name—were in. The amateur dramatics society gave Jean a renewed sense of purpose and Guthrie saw the change it made to her disposition. She spent many evenings with the group and found comfort in the new friends it provided.

Guthrie had eventually confronted his wife about his suspicions. Jean didn't even try to conceal the truth and told him she had been seeing... the other man... for some six months. Deep down Guthrie hoped that his suspicions were wrong but knew the truth before Jean confirmed it. He bottled it up until one evening he made his way to the rehearsal hall, walked up on stage, and clobbered him on the jaw, knocking him on his backside, and sending Jean into an embarrassed rage.

From that night he had never gone back to the house and his contact with Jean had been restricted to phone calls and the occasional meeting to discuss the divorce.

"Tom?"

Hearing his name, made Guthrie snap back to the

present. "Sorry, Ian. Mind on other things for a second there." Guthrie took a seat across from Buchanan and folded his arms. "You were saying?"

Buchanan let out a sigh. "Tom, you have to get your mind back on the issues at hand."

"Aye, I know, sorry."

"It's not good enough just saying you're sorry. I've no idea where your brain is most of the time." Guthrie just shrugged and counted the pencils in the mug on Buchanan's desk. "You know what almost everyone in CID is saying about your performance lately?"

Guthrie rolled his eyes and looked up at the ceiling. "Ian, I know I've been... distracted of late-"

"Distracted! Hell, Tom, there are times on this case I wondered if you knew what day it was, let alone know what we were trying to accomplish."

"I know, I know." Guthrie stood up and walked over to the window overlooking the street at the front of the building. He rubbed his eyes and then ran his fingers through his hair. Turning to face Buchanan he leaned back against the window sill.

"Tom, you got us a result by getting young Mr Davidson to spill the beans about what he knew. However..."

Guthrie knew it was coming. He could feel the blood rise and begin to turn the back of his neck red. "Look, I know what you're going to say and I don't want to hear it." He held up both hands in surrender.

"That may be, Tom, but the fact of the matter is I am responsible for this case. I am your senior officer, as much as that pains you." Guthrie's raised eyebrows were the only giveaway he agreed with Buchanan's statement. "And you are walking a fine line between barely getting the job done and screwing up this entire investigation."

"Aw, come off it, Ian."

"No, Tom. Come off it, *Sir*. This is an official bollocking. I've been told to keep an eye on you and that's just what I intend to do. You better make sure I have no reason to take this conversation further—either with you, or with our superiors."

Guthrie looked at his shoes and folded his arms. "Fine."

"Fine...?"

"Fine... *Inspector* Buchanan."

FIVE

Franky Davidson had provided his interviewers with the story as he knew it. Jock Bishop's girlfriend was the ex of a local thug who did not take too kindly to being dumped in favor of Bishop. It so happened that Franky was sitting at the bar of the nightclub the night Bishop and his girlfriend were out on the town. He spotted them from his barstool perch overlooking the dance floor and called his friend, David Langfeld, to let him know that he'd spotted the couple. Franky knew this would push Langfeld over the edge. He was right.

Langfeld "lost his heid," according to Franky, and demanded to know when they were leaving. Franky asked why but was told it was none of his business, at which point Langfeld hung up.

Before the couple left the club, however, Langfeld showed up with two friends, found a corner booth away from Bishop and the girl—and watched.

According to Franky, as soon as Bishop left, Langfeld and his cronies quickly followed, with Langfeld saying he was going to leave Bishop in no doubt that going out with *his* girl was not on.

When Guthrie had asked Franky what exactly that meant, Franky simply responded, "beat the shite out o' 'im."

It was good enough for Buchanan and Guthrie. It was all they needed to head to the north side of the city with a couple of uniforms following behind in a marked police car.

Langfeld lived on the Trinity council estate. It had seen better days. The three high-rise blocks of flats sat in a shallow crescent facing south. The lower flats looked out towards the industrial park down the hill, but the ones occupying the top floors had a view all the way across the River Tay to Fife. The late sixties design of the towers was not helped by the lack of care the local authority seemed to be providing in the way of upkeep. Paint peeled from almost every surface. the white harling was coming away in patches exposing the prefabricated concrete slabs that made up the basic structure of the building. Pigeons were nesting in broken light fixtures and their guano was everywhere.

"Jeez, what a dump," observed Guthrie as they climbed the four flights of stairs to Langfeld's flat as, to no-one's surprise, the lift was out of order. "I haven't been to this estate for years."

"How did you manage to avoid this place, Tom? Almost every hoodlum in the city either comes from here, has family here, or knows someone here." Buchanan was bringing up the rear, trying not to touch the walls or metal banister, with Guthrie leading the way and the two uniforms between them.

"Somehow I always cornered who I needed to when they were at work, at the pub, or just faffing around down the shops."

"Come off it, Tom. You never had to do what we're

doing now? Come up here and experience their home sweet home?"

"Now, I didn't say I never had to come up here, I just said I hadn't been here for years. I got smart after the first few times. I hated being on their patch, so to speak. Makes you feel like the entire resident population of the building is listening or about to jump you just for being a cop."

They had reached the landing of the fourth floor and stopped to take in the view. Buchanan joined Guthrie at the railing. The evening light made the fields in the far distance look like a painting. Subtle greens and yellows under a perfect, pale blue sky.

"You know, the view's not that bad, is it?" offered Buchanan.

"Nope."

"Shame it has to be wasted on the likes of the folks here, though."

"Oh, aye, Inspector? What a terrible thing to say about the kind people of the Trinity Estate."

Buchanan knocked on the door of Langfeld's flat. Guthrie was still leaning on the railing looking northeast along the coast. He could just make out Broughty Ferry Castle. His own flat was a minute's walk from the old guardian of the Tay estuary.

Buchanan knocked again. "Mr Langfeld?"

After a few seconds the noise of a lock being turned and a latch chain being slid out of its slot could be heard from the other side of the dirty, baby blue door. It opened and Langfeld stood there in Nike trainers, torn jeans and a black t-shirt sporting a skull and proclaiming the wearer would apparently die than live other than free.

"Mr Langfeld, I'm Detective Inspector Buchanan. I wonder if we could have a quick word."

Langfeld looked at Buchanan, taking him in from top to bottom. He assessed the two uniformed officers and glanced at Guthrie, who was still admiring the view.

"Well, come in." He pushed the door open against the wall of the narrow entrance hall and stood there as the others filed passed. "Just go straight on through to the living room," he said as Guthrie, the last in line, entered. Guthrie flashed Langfeld a knowing smile and winked at him.

When Guthrie had reached the door to the kitchen, about half way along the hall, he said, "Nice view you've got here." He turned only to see the door being pulled shut from the outside.

"Bugger!"

"What? What is it?" Buchanan shouted from the living room.

"He's done a runner."

"Shit." Buchanan pushed his way passed the uniforms and yelled at Guthrie, "Well don't just stand there, get after him!"

Guthrie turned the handle and pulled, but the door didn't move. He tugged at it wondering why.

"He's latched the lock," Buchanan shouted, his anger increasing with every second still stuck in the flat.

"Aaaach!" Guthrie fumbled with the small knob on the lock with one hand and kept turning the handle with the other until finally the door opened.

The three men were so close behind him in the cramped hall that he had to force Buchanan back who, in turn, shoved the officer behind him in order to open the door wide enough to spill out onto the landing. Buchanan charged out through the doorway and immediately made the right turn back towards the stairwell.

"Come on!"

SEVEN

By the time the four officers had made it to the ground floor Langfeld was nowhere to be seen. Buchanan ordered the two uniform officers to split up and head to each end of the building. Guthrie and Buchanan surveyed the area directly in front of the block of flats. It looked like half an acre of waste ground.

"Brilliant!"

" He could be anywhere, Ian."

"Really?" Buchanan couldn't contain his anger and frustration. "Damn it, Tom, how did you let him just run out like that?"

"How did I...? Now wait just a minute!"

"No, no, you're right, sorry. We were sucker-punched, that's for sure." Buchanan let out another loud grunt. "He really could be anywhere couldn't he? He could be half a mile away down some street, or in someone's flat."

"Aye," was all Guthrie could say.

"Well, he must know why we're knocking on his door. That stinks of a guilty conscience."

The two uniformed officers returned with the news that

they had found no sign of Langfeld. Guthrie looked up at the looming, greyness of the flats and smiled to himself. Yes, Langfeld had given them the slip all too easily, but Buchanan was right. Why run if you had nothing to worry about? They had him and it was because he had wrung out young Franky.

EIGHT

They picked up Langfeld the next morning and brought him in to the station. He was escorted to an interview room on the second floor. Buchanan and Guthrie faced him across a well-worn table. Langfeld, average height, slim, mid-twenties, short, dark hair with out-of-a bottle highlights, sat slumped down in his chair, shoulders almost level with the top of the chair back, legs stretched out under the table. His arms were folded. The body language said, *screw you.* A uniformed officer stood stoically next to the door.

The interview was not going well, as far as Buchanan was concerned. Langfeld denied he had anything to do with the beating of Jock Bishop.

"Look, you're right, I wasn't happy that Donna was going out with that twat, Bishop."

"And you took it upon yourself to teach him a lesson," Buchanan stated.

"No."

"Yes, you did. And that lesson ended in his death."

"Look, I had nothing to do with it."

"You're lying, Langfeld, and we know it," said Guthrie.

Langfeld leaned forward. "Then you're the one who's making stuff up because I - had - nothing - to - do - with - it." He held Guthrie's stare until it was broken by Guthrie who stood up and walked around behind him. Langfeld resumed his slouched pose.

"We have a witness who says you were going to teach him a lesson," said Buchanan, "and I think you and a couple of your mates followed him once he'd seen Donna home and jumped him as he was cutting through the park."

Langfeld just smirked and shook his head. "You've no idea, have you? You really have no clue? I wasn't anywhere near that park last night - or any night for that matter. I was having a drink with my mates and went home about midnight."

Guthrie, who had propped himself up in the corner of the room, asked, "You can corroborate that, can you?"

"Of course I can. I can give you the names of the lads there. They'll tell you exactly the same story."

"Aye. The same *story*. I bet they can at that."

"And our witness," Buchanan continued, "said he saw you leave the club immediately after Jock and Donna left. Don't you find that a bit of a coincidence?"

"Aye."

"Aye, I bet you do." Guthrie had almost lost his patience. He moved over to Langfeld's left side, bent over until his face was no more than a couple of inches from Langfeld's. "Well, I don't believe in coincidences."

Langfeld's jaw tightened, the muscles moving just below his ear as he ground his teeth together. Guthrie hadn't moved.

"Who was with you? We need the names of your mates you were with," said Buchanan to break the tension.

Langfeld rattled them off in a monotone voice, looking

up at the ceiling. Buchanan made a note of them along with the addresses and mobile phone numbers Langfeld provided and gave the list to Guthrie, telling him to make the calls, before suspending the interview.

"We're going to hold you until we check out your alibi, so get comfy."

"How about a cuppa then?" Langfeld asked. His face a picture of serene innocence. It was as if he was hanging out in the lobby of a hotel, waiting for a friend.

Buchanan nodded to the uniformed officer by the door who was glad for the opportunity to get out of the small, stale room.

"Two sugars if you don't mind," Langfeld called as the door closed.

"Let's see what your friends tell us, shall we?"

Guthrie opened the door and held it ajar as Buchanan walked out.

"Skimmed or almond milk?" Guthrie asked. Langfeld just snorted. Guthrie closed the door behind him, not waiting for an answer.

NINE

Guthrie was dispatched to interview Langfeld's alibis. Both of them recounted the same story; they were indeed in the nightclub that evening, and they did see Bishop and the girl. Langfeld was not happy about it and he wanted to do something to let Bishop know of his displeasure. They left the club and waited close to Bishop's flat, but when he didn't show up, they all went home.

Guthrie wasn't surprised and pushed both of Langfeld's friends hoping they would change their stories just enough that he could catch them in their lies, but each one said the exact same thing as the other.

When Guthrie got back to West Bell Street, he found a table in the canteen and sat down with a coffee and a pie that he had heated in the microwave. He had looked for Buchanan, couldn't find him, so left a note on his desk telling the inspector he was back and where he could be found.

Halfway through his marginal pastry and meat product meal, Buchanan entered the canteen and took a seat at the table.

"Well?"

"Their stories line up with Langfeld's."

"No surprise there."

"Nope. I'll take another shot at them and see if we can't get them to spill the beans."

"Let's bring them in and do this formally. I don't want you pulling another stunt like your chat with Franky Davidson." Buchanan stood up. "I'll get a car to pick them up."

"Fine." Guthrie took another bite of his pie and instantly regretted it. A mouthful of coffee only helped to drown the taste temporarily. It lingered on Guthrie's taste buds like the smell of a wet dog lingers in a room long after it has moved on.

Guthrie felt a knot form in his stomach. Buchanan's words were swirling around in his head.

Stunt.

Standing up he pushed the chair away from the table with the back of his legs. Tossing the half-eaten pie and paper cup into the bin, he followed Buchanan out of the canteen.

TEN

Langfeld's two friends were escorted to West Bell Street but the formal interviews brought nothing new to light. Guthrie signed for a pool car and drove Buchanan to Donna's house.

The 1970s era house was in the middle of a quiet side street off the Kingsway, one of the main arteries running east-west through town.

Donna ushered them into the kitchen where she motioned for them to take a seat at a small table set against one wall. Both officers politely refused and the three of them stood awkwardly around a wooden island on which were stacks of letters, junk mail and various packets of biscuits and crisps.

The young woman was dressed in a navy-blue hoodie and jeans. She was wearing her long, blonde hair in a ponytail, but wore no make-up.

The thirty-minute visit reviewed Donna's and Bishop's movements during their night out. She recounted the events in a quiet but confident voice and looked the officers in the eyes as they asked their questions.

Guthrie and Buchanan heard the same story: Nightclub, walk home, Bishop left.

On the drive back to headquarters Buchanan laid out a possible plan of action going forward - another interview with Langfeld and his mates, stepping up the call for witnesses, another press conference—but Guthrie wasn't listening.

No. There was something just not right about Donna's tone and body language. Buchanan obviously didn't pick up on it and Guthrie wasn't going to share his thoughts.

They were almost back to the station when Guthrie suddenly realised what it was. Of course. Should he tell Buchanan? Yes, he *should*. Guthrie had already made up his mind. As soon as they parked the pool car, he excused himself and walked through the car park and found his own vehicle.

He drove back to Donna's house.

ELEVEN

As Guthrie pulled up in front of Donna's house, the skies were starting to turn a dark blue as late afternoon gave way to early evening. The yellow-orange of the street lights turned the dark stone of the houses a dirty brown color. The street was deserted. The only sign of life was a cat which ran across the road, ducking under a parked car before jumping onto a wall. It looked in Guthrie's direction, then disappeared into a front garden of a house two along the row from where Guthrie was parked.

He turned off the ignition and took a deep breath.

When Donna opened the door her surprise was obvious. She looked around expecting the other officer who had come earlier with the one standing on her doorstep now. She gathered her composure. "Detective Sergeant Guthrie, right?" she said.

"That's right, yes."

"Sorry, wasn't expecting you again."

"I just have a few more questions. May I?"

Donna opened the door further and let Guthrie pass by

her. She closed the door and Guthrie automatically looked behind him. This time, the home owner was still there.

"I just need to go over some things again with you." He made his way back to the kitchen without guidance from Donna. This time he took a seat at the small table, again without the offer from his host.

"I told you everything I know, Mr Guthrie. I'm not sure I can help more."

Guthrie took a breath. The knot in his stomach was there again. It was a nervous feeling. It felt like he was about to jump off the high platform at the swimming pool for the first time when he was a kid. A feeling that made his pulse quicken. He was about to do something that was going to get a result—he knew it. He just had to step off the platform.

"Donna, I want the truth."

"What do you mean? I told you-"

"I know what you *told* me earlier," Guthrie interrupted. He was going to waste no time in getting to the point, "but I think you know something more. I think you know exactly what happened that night." Guthrie held Donna's gaze. The silence seemed to fill the small kitchen. The pause was all Guthrie needed to know he was right. He could feel his heart pounding in his chest. *Gotcha*, he thought to himself.

Donna turned away and busied herself by picking up a dirty coffee mug, turning on the water and washing it before placing it upside-down on a drying rack on the counter.

"I'm sorry you think that, but I told you everything."

"Bollocks!"

Donna turned around quickly. As she spun to face Guthrie her ponytail came around her face looking like it whipped her on the cheek. Her eyes were already filling up with tears of emotion. The emotion wasn't sadness. Guthrie saw it and pushed his attack.

"Donna, you and I both know you lied to me and my colleague earlier, so why don't we start again?"

"I don't know what you're talking about."

"I think you do."

Another silence.

"I'll tell you what I think happened." Donna just looked at him saying nothing. Her head was down slightly so her stare came at Guthrie through the blonde fringe of her hair. "I think it was a set-up. I think you're still very friendly with Mr Langfeld." Donna folded her arms and with a flick of her head moved her ponytail off her shoulder.

"Okay, so not an item, the two of you, but you still have a thing going on. Ask me how I know?" Donna didn't rise to Guthrie's bait, so he continued. "I know because one of Langfeld's mates with him last night was your cousin. So that got me thinking. What if there was something you, your cousin, Langfeld, and Jock Bishop had in common? And you know, that little question niggled away at me from the time we left here this afternoon all the way back to the station. Then it dawned on me, Donna."

Guthrie picked up a bottle from the table. It was small, brown plastic, with a white cap. He shook it and the pills inside rattled. "It really did take me a while to figure it out, Donna, but then it just clicked. I'm afraid I wasn't very good company for DI Buchanan in the car, but I'm sure when I tell him that you had helped to set-up Bishop because he screwed up the little pill-pushing deal you all had, I'm sure he'll understand."

"You're full of it!" Donna yelled. "You're seriously accusing me of... of... murder? I don't have to listen to this. Get out. Get out now!" She pointed, straight-armed towards the front door.

"Come off it, Donna. The four of you were up to your

necks in this deal." Guthrie was standing now and shaking the pill bottle at her.

"You're crazy."

"I don't think so. It's common knowledge around town that you were knocking off chemists and using the stuff to sell on as part of a legal high scam."

"Oh, yeah? If that's true, why haven't we been arrested? Or are you coming to arrest me for that now? I don't think so, Mr Guthrie."

She was right, of course. The police had nothing on them. They were careful and clever. Nothing stuck to them. Sure, plenty of accusations, but not one piece of solid evidence. Just talk, Rumors. But Guthrie could sense she was just dying to say it was all true and the cops had nothing on them. So, he pushed.

"Ach, you're right, Donna. You and your mates are all probably too thick to be that smart. Too stupid to out-fox the polis, eh? Poor, dumb coppers, but you're even dumber. And what's more, your ex is using you, just like you're using those poor slobs you sell this crap to." Guthrie threw the bottle down at Donna's feet. It hit the fake hardwood linoleum floor splitting the bottle open. Small, white pills spilled out and slid in all directions.

"You just don't see it, Donna. You're nothing to Langfeld. He used you and probably moved onto a prettier girl. He used you to get back at Bishop. You've fulfilled your purpose and now he's just going to throw you away. You helped him get back at Bishop and he just couldn't care less."

"NO!" screamed Donna. The outburst was like an explosion. Spit flew from her mouth like the lava from a volcano's peak. "No! Jock Bishop betrayed us, and he had to be taught a lesson. He thought he could go it alone and take over what we had built up. He thought he was better than the rest of us."

"That's crap, Donna. You're not smart enough for revenge." Guthrie was feeding the flames of her anger. He was making up the stuff on the fly. He really had no clue if he was close to the truth. He knew, however, that if he could just keep her angry the whole story will come out.

"Not smart enough? You really are a shite. I'm smarter than the lot of them." She walked over to Guthrie as she spoke. Her face was scarlet. "I'm smarter than you." She poked him in the chest. She was only a few inches shorter than Guthrie. He hadn't noticed how tall she was before.

"I knew I could get the boys to help me. I knew I could get them to keep quiet."

"How did it feel?

"What?" The question seemed to break her thinking.

"How did it feel to kick the life out of him?"

She breathed in noisily through her nose. "How do you think? He had it coming to him."

Gotcha.

"But you still had to enlist the help of the men, eh? Couldn't do it on your own, poor little girly."

By the time Guthrie realized she was swinging at him, the punch had already connected to his gut. Out of pure reflex he bent forward and instinctively wrapped his arms in front of him. Donna lifted her knee and caught him between the legs. Guthrie groaned and let fly with his right hand, swinging backhanded in an upward arc from his left side. It connected under her chin and she staggered back to the sink.

Guthrie straightened up. "Bugger. Bugger," was all he could manage.

Donna was bleeding from her lip. "Get out!" she screamed.

Guthrie said nothing. He walked slowly out of the kitchen.

Outside, the light had almost all but gone. The street was still void of life. A good thing, he thought to himself. He didn't want to be seen walking gingerly to his car. He unlocked the door, opened it and slumped into the seat. He took a napkin out of the glove compartment and wiped the sweat from his forehead and neck. He turned the key in the ignition. He was sore, but he smiled to himself.

"Gotcha."

TWELVE

Guthrie's mobile phone beeped and vibrated on the table beside his bed. He reached for it to turn off the alarm he had set the night before. His stomach still ached from Donna's punch the previous evening.

As he picked up the phone he saw it wasn't the alarm, but a call. Buchanan's name was on the screen. "Good morning. You're on the go early."

"Get your arse in here right now. I'll be waiting for you in the ground floor conference room."

A series of short beeps told Guthrie Buchanan had already hung up.

"Bugger."

He slowly stood and walked into the bathroom. He brushed his teeth, shaved and showered. The suit he had worn the day before was hanging on the door of his bedroom closet. He quickly ironed a white shirt and dressed.

All the time he was thinking about Donna's confession and that he would be able to report that back to Buchanan this morning, but the phone call had muddied the water of his morning plan. What could be so important that Buchanan was already at the station?

He grabbed a tie and his keys and made sure he put his phone in the inside pocket of his jacket and made his way outside and to his car.

The sun was just coming up over the hills on the other side of the river as he backed out of the space and started on the fifteen-minute drive to West Bell Street. He turned on the radio to the local station. The news report was on. He punched a few more preset buttons before finding some music. He didn't recognize the band, but it sounded good, so he settled there.

Traffic was relatively light, and he hit all the traffic lights with perfect timing. As he made the turn into the car park he thought that might be a record for his commute—probably a good two minutes shorter than normal.

Through the floor to ceiling glass panels making up the long wall that separated the conference room from the main hallway and the various offices opposite, Guthrie could see Buchanan pacing back and forth behind a long, mahogany table. He had barely stepped into the room when Buchanan greeted him.

"You're in deep shit, pal."

"What? Sorry, what have I done? I just walked in the door?"

"What have you done?" Buchanan could barely keep his anger in check. His cheeks were flushed, and patches of red were visible on his neck, just above his collar. "You've only just screwed yourself, me and may have jeopardized the entire investigation, that's what."

"I'm sorry, what are you talking about?"

"How was your chat with Donna yesterday evening?"

Guthrie's mind started racing. How did he know about his visit with Donna?

"Who told you I talked with her?"

"Ha!" Buchanan threw his head back in a mock belly laugh. "*Talked* to her? That's a laugh. I received a call at six this morning from the Chief Super, asking for my presence in his office at seven. Needless to say, I was a little flummoxed as to what that may be about but I was pretty sure it was not to ask how my holiday went."

"Oh."

"Aye, *oh*. Imagine my surprise when he told me that a complaint had come in first thing this morning about an officer assaulting Jock Bishop's girlfriend?"

"She confessed to being there. She confessed to setting the whole thing up."

"We know she was there."

Guthrie wasn't sure he heard what Buchanan said. He screwed his eyes shut and shook his head. He could hear the blood roaring in his ears as the sudden silence in the room enveloped him.

"What did you say?"

"We know she was there. We know she was at the scene."

"Wha-?" Guthrie still had his eyes shut. His brain seemed to be going everywhere and nowhere at the same time.

"Scenes of Crime had gathered up everything lying around the scene which included a lipstick. The lipstick matched traces found on Bishop's lips and cheek. The park is not on the way from the nightclub to her house, so they wouldn't have walked through there on the way. It *is* on the way from her house to Bishop's flat."

"When did you find this out?"

"Yesterday morning."

"Yesterday... Why didn't you tell me? Why didn't you share that piece of information with me?" Guthrie's confusion was quickly turning to anger. "Why, Ian?"

"Because you didn't need to know."

"I didn't need to know? Am I part of this investigation or not?"

"Tom, you've barely been part of this investigation from the outset. How many times since we were assigned to this case have you been told to get with it? I had to remind you just the other day."

"But that doesn't excuse you from holding back information critical to the case. What are you trying to do?"

"I'm not trying to do anything, Tom. You're managing to do quite nicely on your own. Just like yesterday's visit to Donna."

Buchanan had made his way around the end of the conference table towards Guthrie who was still only two steps inside the room.

"You have, for whatever reason, decided that you know better. You know what and how things should be handled and all without consulting me or anyone else for that matter." He kept coming towards Guthrie who tensed, not sure what to expect. "Your methods are not how we do things. We have policies and procedures designed to maximize the effort of the team and keep us out of trouble with lawyers. Your little excursion to Donna's yesterday was the last straw, Tom. You've been suspended with immediate effect, pending an investigation of your actions with respect to your conduct and treatment of Franky Davidson and Donna Shepherd."

"Och, come off it, Ian- "

"*Inspector!*"

"Ach!" Guthrie grabbed the nearest chair and shoved it hard against the table.

"Go home, Tom. I don't want to see you until I need you to sign some paperwork. It doesn't look good from where I'm standing."

"I bet it doesn't, 'cos from where I'm standing it feels like a bit of a stitch-up."

"You stitched yourself up, Tom."

"Aye, right." Guthrie turned to see half a dozen faces peering through the glass from the hall. The shouting had sparked some interest from the clerical staff in the offices. Guthrie hadn't even closed the conference room door before the argument had begun so the commotion had penetrated several offices in both directions.

He didn't take the time to wonder what they had heard, but slowly walked past them, down the hall and through a side door that spilled him out on one end of the car park. He turned to head back in and tell Buchanan exactly what he thought of the man. Swiping his ID badge against the electronic lock he opened the door.

He let his head fall, chin almost touching his chest. *What's the use*, he thought to himself. He let the door swing closed and walked back to his car.

The interior was still warm from the short drive not ten minutes before. He put the key in the ignition but didn't turn it. He let his head fall back against the headrest and closed his eyes.

"You've done it this time, Tom," he said to himself.

THIRTEEN

The sun was setting.

Guthrie looked out of the window of his flat. The view was a little better than the one he had admired almost three months prior from the fourth floor of the Trinity estate. The sky above the hills across the Tay estuary were clothed in a golden hue. The river itself was the darkest blue, almost black, in color.

To his left, the water in the harbor between his flat and Broughty Ferry Castle was calm and sheltered a couple of small boats. A flag on the pole perched on the highest point of the castle's main tower fluttered in the light breeze.

To Guthrie's right he could make out the lights of the traffic on the road bridge, crossing from Tayside to the Kingdom of Fife heading, perhaps, to St. Andrews, Kirkcaldy, or further; across the Forth and to Edinburgh and beyond.

Immediately below his window a young couple slowly made their way arm-in-arm along the sea wall. They were eating ice cream, presumably from the shop just around the corner from the flat. Their pace was slow, admiring the same view and enjoying the warmth of the summer evening.

Guthrie took a sip of coffee and held the mug in both hands. Its hot surface seemed to radiate from his hands all the way up his arms. He shivered and realized he was staring, unfocused, at the small waves breaking on the pebble beach beyond the wall.

There had been many evenings like this over the past few weeks since he officially retired from the force. Not that it was his choice. The heavy-handed tactics he had used with Donna and Franky were all the senior officers needed to convince him that it would be in his best interest, and the interest of Tayside Police, if he quietly retired. Doing so saved both parties the embarrassment of a lengthy inquiry as a result of his non-standard policing methods.

At first, he was angry. He was convinced that Buchanan had deliberately engineered his downfall but thinking about it over and over again he came to the conclusion he was his own chief engineer. The Chief Super had been somewhat apologetic but had told Guthrie that his hands were tied. He was sympathetic to his side of the story but, "We just can't do things like that anymore, Tom," he had said.

Ironically, in the end it mattered not. They had all the evidence they needed to tie Donna to the scene and build a case against her. The truth would eventually have come out and Donna, Langfeld, and the others would have been locked up. Guthrie should have played the game, but he went off on his own.

By the time he drove away from West Bell Street for the last time, he had convinced himself that it was actually a blessing in disguise. He was not like the new crop of cops they were churning out: young, eager, motivated, university graduates, full of ideals and desires to climb the promotion ladder.

No, he was certainly none of those things. A blessing in disguise.

The icing on the cake was that his divorce from Jean was finalised less than two weeks after his last day on the force.

So here I am, he thought to himself, *middle-aged, divorced, unemployed. What now?*

He walked over to the kitchen counter and refilled his mug with more coffee. He stirred in a spoonful of sugar, some milk, and returned to the window.

At least I have a decent view.

But so do the little nyaffs on the Trinity estate.

Suddenly he felt tired, as if the past three months had decided to crash down on him all at once. He felt completely wrung out.

"Ach, bugger."

MURDER IN THE
SMA' GLEN

ONE

RESOLUTIONS

It was a vicious evening. The storm was ripping through the glen with effortless power. Trees that had stood as markers in the landscape for centuries were forced to give up their stance and crashed down in submission to the unseen force of the wind. Roads were blocked with debris. Powerlines were down. The entire country had come to a virtual standstill.

The rain fell in sheets, driven and whipped by the wind. It drummed against the windows of the Foulford Inn, a small white-washed building sitting just off the road, alone in the middle of the Sma' Glen.

Tom Guthrie, a middle-aged, retired detective sergeant, sat at the bar. He nursed a glass of whisky. There was something about an evening like this that demanded a log fire and a whisky—and tonight he had both.

He should have been back home after deciding to take a break from his flat for the weekend. Dusting off the mountain bike and securing it to the rack on the back of his car, he set off to discover some quiet country roads. It had been one of his New Year's resolutions, and he thought he'd better make a start on it.

It was early October.

Rather than drive the relatively short distance back home at the end of the day, he figured he'd find somewhere to spend the night. Not going back to his flat in Broughty Ferry would make it feel more like a holiday. He had packed a small suitcase, and stopped at the tourist information office in Crieff. The young lady behind the desk gave him brochures outlining the amenities of various hotels, and he decided on the Foulford Inn. Located on a quiet secondary road between Crieff to the west and Perth to the east, it afforded easy access to some good cycling roads.

So here he was: sore back, tired legs and a raw backside. He couldn't imagine what he'd be like after his second day on the bike.

As he pondered just how fast his body had given up being in its 20s and acclimatised to being in its 40s, the flames from the fire reflected in the tumbler in his hand. He swirled the golden liquid around in the glass. It had been three months to the day that he had retired from Tayside Police. He raised the glass.

Cheers, he thought. *Here's to you, Tom, you old bugger. What are you like?*

Sipping the peaty blend, he smiled inwardly at his own cleverness. The day before, as part of his cycling plans, he had stopped for lunch at Glenturret Distillery. After taking the guided tour, several items from the gift shop were safely stowed in his backpack, including a bottle of *The Black Grouse*, for the short ride back to the Foulford.

Today had been a bust. The storm had swept in from Iceland and enveloped the country with hurricane-force winds. Guthrie wished he had planned a little better and checked the forecast before deciding to spend two days outside, but as usual, he had something stuck in his head, and he was going to do it, come hell or...

He had spent the day sitting in the bar reading and chatting with the locals. The Inn had its own golf course, and the few regulars who had turned up despite the weather had proven to be welcome and interesting company. Dinner was a traditional offering of steak pie, thick chips, vegetables, all washed down with a pint of lager. Now he was feeling the effects of a lazy day, a meal that completely negated any good he had done on the bike the day before, and a good nip o' whisky.

It had just gone 7pm. Guthrie had put the *Grouse* away and was sampling the beers on draught and chatting with the barmaid, Jen, the hotel owner's daughter. She was in her 20s, short dark hair, and dressed casually in jeans and a grey sweatshirt. The bar was quiet now that the locals had all gone home. Whether it was because of the storm or the usual way of things at the Foulford, Guthrie didn't know. Beyond the gale outside, the only noise was of the logs crackling and spitting in the fire, and the ticking of a small clock on the wall behind the bar.

"It's funny, isn't it?"

"What is?"

Guthrie nodded towards the large windows which, during the day, afforded a view of the now dark golf course behind the hotel. "Small talk always includes the topic of the weather, and here we are in the middle of the biggest storm in years, and we haven't even mentioned it once this evening."

"Aye, you're right," Jen smiled, "but talking about whisky and beer is much better." Jen pulled a clean pint glass from under the counter and wiggled it questioningly towards Guthrie.

"Why not?" Guthrie said after a moment's thought. He finished the last inch in his glass. Jen had been kind enough to let Guthrie sneak his whisky into the bar earlier and had even provided the glass, so he felt an appropriate response should be to at least have a couple of pints after dinner.

Jen went over to the taps at the far end of the bar. As she slowly pulled the pint down the side of the glass, the quiet was destroyed by the door at the end of the room crashing open. Both Guthrie and Jen were startled and looked out of reflex towards the noise. A man staggered in. He didn't bother closing the door behind him, and the rain was blown through the opening by the gale still raging in the darkness.

"Close the door, mate," Guthrie called across the room.

The man appeared not to hear, and unsteadily made his way towards the bar. He was in his 60s and dressed in brown corduroy trousers, and Barbour jacket. He had a ruddy complexion. Guthrie thought he looked like a farmer.

"The door!" Guthrie repeated and pointed over the man's shoulder. The new arrival was soaked from head to foot. It was raining hard, but you didn't get that wet making your way from the small car park to the building. The man continued walking towards Guthrie.

As he passed Jen, she let out a short shriek. She saw that his face wasn't red from being outside but from the blood pouring down the side of his head. He didn't make it another step. He fell to his knees, catching himself on a barstool before collapsing to the floor.

"Bloody hell!" Guthrie exclaimed. He jumped off his barstool and knelt down at the man's side. There was a deep gash above his ear. Blood was pouring down the right side of the man's head as much as the rain was pouring outside.

"Quick, Jen, I need a towel."

She grabbed a couple of clean bar towels and ran around to kneel beside the stranger.

"Here, prop his head up and clean off his face."

Guthrie could see that the wound was in poor shape. He fished his cell phone from the front pocket of his jeans and dialled 999.

"Hello, yes, we need an ambulance at the Foulford Inn just outside Crieff on the A822." The emergency operator asked some questions and Guthrie answered them— description of the victim, extent of the injuries—all the while holding a towel to the man's head to stop the bleeding. He handed the phone to Jen when the operator asked about a contact phone number and the address of the hotel.

Jen gave the information then ended the call. "They said it might be thirty minutes before they can get here. The ambulance is coming from Perth. And who knows what the roads are like, the weather the way it is."

"Thirty minutes? Jeez."

The man opened his eyes and moaned. He was trying to say something. Guthrie leaned forward so he was directly over him. "It's okay, pal. Just lie there."

"He... He..." He groaned and reached for the side of his head.

"Easy." Guthrie took his hand and immediately felt the man's grasp. It was strong, taking Guthrie by surprise.

"He hit... me."

"Who hit you?"

"He stopped, came at me and..." The man closed his eyes. It seemed that it was everything he could do to get the words out.

"Take your time." Guthrie looked up at Jen. Her face was a complex mix of concern and fright.

"Hit me. I tried to drive... Flat tyre... About a mile back..." The man tried to push against the floor as if he was trying to sit up.

"Easy," Guthrie repeated. "You just lie there."

"What the hell?"

The voice belonged to the hotel's owner, Jim Lawson. The big man was standing just inside the doorway, the rain blowing in behind him. Guthrie's mind wondered when the lightning would flash like some low-budget thriller movie. Guthrie shook the thought from his head. Jim had been working in his garage when he had looked up and spotted the open door to the bar and decided to find out what was going on.

"Dad!" Jen stood up and ran over to him. "He just walked in. He's been hit on the head."

"Okay, sweetheart." Jim wrapped his arms around his daughter as she buried her head into his chest. She started to sob.

Guthrie refocused his attention on the man lying beside him. The white bar towel was quickly--too quickly--turning bright red.

"I need the other towel," he said, pointing at the second one Jen had brought from behind the bar. It was lying on the floor on the other side of the man, just out of Guthrie's reach. He didn't want to release the pressure from the wound.

"I'll get it," said Lawson. He stepped forward as Jen released her grip on him. Kneeling down, he picked up the towel and handed it to Guthrie.

"Thanks."

"What happened?"

"Not exactly sure. He said something about a flat tyre and someone hitting him. Do you know him?"

Lawson gave a non-committal nod of the head. "I've seen him in town, but don't know him."

"He's not one of your regulars?"

"No."

"Do you know his name?"

"No." Lawson's brow furrowed. "I think he may be one of the gillies on the Aberalmond Estate."

"Aberalmond?" Guthrie had seen the large, gated entrance the day before on his way back from Glenturret. "That's the big estate on the north side of the road, isn't it? You think he works for them?"

"Aye. I'm not sure, though. Like I said, I've never seen him in here before."

"What's your name?" Guthrie asked the man, who was now lying still, eyes closed. His breathing was slow, steady, but shallow. Guthrie was becoming more concerned as the minutes passed. The man didn't answer. Blood was still seeping steadily into the towel. It didn't appear to be slowing.

"Where's that bloody ambulance?" he spat. "Jim, is there anyone locally who could get here quicker than coming from Perth?" Jim Lawson rubbed his cheek and thought for a second. "A doctor in Crieff perhaps?"

Lawson stood up and turned towards Jen. "Call Doc Haig, Jen. See if he's in town." Then, turning back to Guthrie, "He's a regular here. Plays golf about once a week."

"Good," said Guthrie. He then searched for something that could tell him more about the man lying on the floor of the bar. Unzipping the man's jacket he found it in the left, inside pocket. He unfolded the small leather wallet and pulled out a credit card.

"Alexander Chambers. Ring any bells?"

"No," Lawson responded.

Guthrie looked up at Jen who had leaned over the bar, found the number of the doctor in the club registry and dialled it. She held the phone to her ear with one hand and with the other was gripping the back of a barstool looking for all the world like she would crumple to the floor if she let go.

"Any luck?"

Jen shook her head. "Answering machine." She waited until the greeting had ended and left a short message urging the doctor to come immediately to the Foulford.

"Bugger," Guthrie said to no-one in particular, then, "Mr. Chambers? Mr. Chambers, can you hear me?"

The man didn't respond. The blood was still flowing freely, and the second towel was now well and truly soaked through. Guthrie looked up at Lawson.

"Got another?"

Lawson walked behind the bar and came back with two more towels. Guthrie swapped his for a clean one, tossing the one stained and heavy with blood to the side.

"Mr. Chambers?" Guthrie gently shook the man's arm as he said his name. Nothing. The noise of the rain and wind suddenly filled the room. It had been there since Chambers had stumbled in, but Guthrie had tuned it out as he concentrated on what to do. Jen sniffed back some more tears.

Cradling the man's arm in his, Guthrie tried to find a pulse. After fifteen seconds or so, he was still trying to find it.

"I can't find a pulse, and his breathing is very shallow. Where is that ambulance?" Guthrie said quietly but through gritted teeth.

Chambers suddenly opened his eyes and took a deep, noisy breath. It took Guthrie by surprise. Chambers groaned as the breath slowly escaped from his lungs. His heart skipped a beat. Then another. Then another. Then there were no more beats left to skip.

Guthrie put a hand on the man's chest. He couldn't feel any movement. He then held his hand barely above Chamber's mouth with his index finger just below his nose. He couldn't feel the slightest hint of breath. He leaned forward and put his ear to the man's chest and looked along his body. He heard nothing and saw that his chest was not rising and falling. One more attempt to find a pulse in both wrists and his neck.

Nothing.

Jim Lawson knew the man had died. Saying nothing he walked over to the door and closed it. He shut out the howl of the wind as it rushed down the small glen and through the branches of the trees. The noise of the rain hitting the wooden floor of the bar just inside the door faded as the door was closed. The swirling of the air also stopped. All three of them were so used to the noise and wind over the last few minutes its sudden disappearance felt like the whole world had just stopped.

Jen started to cry again, this time she didn't hold back. The sound made Guthrie shiver. Jim Lawson was standing by the door, one hand resting on the handle, head slightly bowed.

Guthrie slumped back on his heals. He noticed where he was kneeling, water and blood were beginning to mix in little pools around Chamber's head. The metronomic ticking of the small clock behind the bar seemed to grow louder. It filled the void left when Chamber's heart stopped beating.

THREE

WHY?

Not long after Alexander Chambers died, the Foulford Inn became a much busier place.

Guthrie had placed another 999 call and relayed to the operator what Chambers had said before he passed away. It seemed that he'd been hit on the head by someone. Now he was dead. Someone needed to investigate why.

They arrived within the hour, struggling through the wind and driving rain to reach the small whitewashed hotel. The ambulance pulled into the car park first, the paramedics then waited until the police arrived to make sure of what they needed to do since the death was suspicious. Two uniformed police officers were next to arrive, closely followed by a pair of detectives.

Guthrie didn't know them. They were from Perth, a different division of Tayside Police than his old assignment in Dundee. Introductions were made and Guthrie gave them a summary of the events so far, including Chamber's last few words about what had happened to him in the dark of the storm. The two officers listened intently, one making notes in a small black book. When Guthrie had finished, they thanked him and asked if he was going to be staying on at the hotel.

"Yes, I'll be around. I was planning on checking-out just after lunch."

"Thank you, Mr Guthrie. Someone'll have to talk to you again in the morning to get a formal statement, but we'll get a message to you."

Guthrie didn't let on he was a retired cop and was thoroughly familiar with the routine. He smiled politely and told them he was available at any time.

The two detectives turned their attention to Jim and Jen Lawson. They were standing behind the bar, Jim with one arm around his daughter. For the first time, Guthrie realised he had not seen a Mrs Lawson and wondered where she was, if indeed she was still in the picture. Jen looked like she had been crying for a solid hour. Her eyes were red. She held a handkerchief in one hand and was wiping her nose every few seconds. Jim Lawson stood, brow furrowed, watching the comings and goings of more police officers and the other professionals as they surveyed the bar taking pictures and making notes. The detectives started their primary interviews of father and daughter together.

Guthrie decided to take a seat in the corner of the bar, furthest away from the main door and closest to the hallway leading to the guest rooms. He could have just as easily gone back to his room, but something inside made him stay. He regarded the activity as if he was sitting watching a documentary on television. He seemed slightly removed from everything, yet he knew he was part of it.

Part of it.

He wasn't part of it. Not in the way he was used to. He was usually the one interviewing witnesses, assessing the scene, trying to work out who, what, where, when, why, and how.

Why? The single word seemed to float in the middle of his head, somewhere behind his eyes. He felt he could close them and he would see the word in stark, white relief against a black void. Why did Alexander Chambers die? Who whacked him on the head? Question after question surfaced in his mind. What happened out in that storm less than two hours ago?

Guthrie stared at the floor. Not looking at anything in particular, everything was out of focus. He suddenly realised and looked up to see Alexander Chambers being placed in a black body bag. The oversized zip seemed to make an unrealistically loud noise as it was fastened by the paramedic. The bag was placed on a gurney to be wheeled out to the ambulance.

Guthrie stood up, caught Lawson's eye, and motioned that he was going back to his room. Lawson nodded. Jen was no longer in the bar. She must have gone while Guthrie's mind was off somewhere else. He hadn't noticed. Before he left, he looked back and saw Lawson bring a mop and bucket from a closet at the end of the bar. He rolled it over to where Chambers had been lying and started to clean up the blood.

FOUR

WHAT?

Back in his room, Guthrie washed out a glass and poured himself a healthy measure of *The Black Grouse*. He took a generous mouthful and grimaced after swallowing the straight whisky. He poured some more into the glass, took a pillow, sat down in the one armchair in the room, putting his feet up on the edge of the bed. He placed the oversized pillow behind his head and nestled back into it. It felt cool. Pillow temperatures: one of the great mysteries of the world.

The room around him was still, but the wind continued to drive the rain against the window. The storm was supposed to blow over during the night. Perhaps he could get out in the morning and take a ride on his bike before he had to check out. Closing his eyes, he saw the pained face of Alexander Chambers.

He felt tired. The alcohol from earlier in the evening had been overpowered by adrenalin when Chambers had wrecked the peace of the bar. In the quiet of his room, events were catching up with him. He opened his eyes and looked at the glass in his hand. He took another mouthful.

"What happened to you, Mr. Chambers?"

FIVE

GUTHRIE'S SECRET

The next morning Guthrie was up and in the small breakfast room just as the sun started to appear from behind the hills beyond the golf course. It was as if the weather had decided to ignore what it did to the country the day before and was on its best behaviour. It was one of those mornings when you knew the rest of the day was going to be glorious.

Guthrie passed on the full cooked breakfast of eggs, sausages, beans, bacon, fried tomatoes, and black pudding and stuck with a bowl of oatmeal washed down with a large glass of orange juice and a cup of coffee.

"How are you this morning?" The question came from Jim Lawson. He was standing in the door of the room and sporting a blue and white striped apron.

"Oh, I'm fine. How are you?"

"Okay."

"And Jen? She looked a little fragile when I last saw her."

"She'll survive," her father said. He walked over to a table and picked up the dirty plates.

"Look, I'm sorry all that happened last night. I know it's

the last thing you want—police cars and an ambulance parked outside--and... well... everything that went on inside." Guthrie looked down at the bowl on the table in front of him.

"Not your fault, Mr. Guthrie."

"I know, but... you know..."

Lawson stacked two coffee cups onto the plates balanced in the crook of his arm.

"Well, I'm off to see if my backside will stand another couple of hours on a bike." He stood up and headed for the door. "If the boys in blue want to see me, tell them I'll be back before lunch at the latest."

"Thanks, Mr Guthrie."

"For what?"

"I can't imagine what it would have been like if you weren't there last night and Jen was alone in the bar. I was messing around in the garage. I should have been working, not her." He leaned with one hand on the table. His back was towards Guthrie, his head bowed.

"Just been the two of us since her mum walked out on us a dozen years ago."

"I can't imagine. Single dad. Working hard every day, keeping the hotel going. Being the sole parent of a young woman."

Lawson turned. "She's been great. I just get very protective of her, and something like last night was well beyond my experience level. There are times when I just don't know what to say. I want her to know I'm always going to be there for her. Does that make sense?"

Guthrie smiled and nodded.

"I don't mind telling you, it's not been easy."

"You've done a brilliant job, Jim. Anyone can see that.

And what happened last night is beyond everybody's normal routine."

"Yes, but you seemed to know what to do."

"Little secret." Guthrie walked back towards Lawson. Stopping, he looked around as if he were about to confide in Lawson something no-one on the planet should know. He leaned in and whispered, "I'm a retired copper."

A grin slowly spread across Lawson's face. "You bugger. Did you tell them last night?"

"Nope."

"Ha!" Lawson's mood seemed to change in an instant. He walked out, heading for the kitchen.

Guthrie smiled. However difficult he knew it would be, he wanted Lawson to start getting back into a normal routine. He had seen it many times before while in the police, and he understood the recovery process from experiencing something like last night had to start immediately. You had to get the images out of your mind. You had to move on.

But he was one to talk. He wanted to get an early start today, not because he wanted to keep a promise to himself to get out on the bike, but to see first-hand where Alexander Chambers had been attacked.

SIX

A BIKE RIDE

Guthrie's first decision was whether to head east or west out of the car park. He chose east. He didn't know where Chambers had been attacked, but he did know that it was about a mile from the Foulford so if he had chosen incorrectly he could head back the other way and not have to worry about going ten miles in the wrong direction.

It turned out he was right. Just under a mile down the road, he spotted a police car and an unmarked, white van at the junction to a lane leading up the hill away from the main road. Parked on the side road was a dark blue Citroen van.

Guthrie slowed as he approached the scene. The Citroen was facing up the hill. It was parked about twenty feet off the main road, all four wheels on the paved surface. Guthrie figured Chambers had pulled in because of a puncture. He had mentioned something about a flat tyre the night before. He could see the front left was sitting on the rim. The junction had been cordoned off with the obligatory police tape, and a uniformed officer was trying not to look utterly bored, wondering why he had to stand outside rather than sit in the car. Three other people were kneeling or crouching over various spots around the blue van or the road. A fourth was in the field just the other side of a low hedge. All of them were wearing white over-suits, and booties covered their shoes.

"Morning," Guthrie called out to the lone uniformed officer. He came to a stop beside him. Guthrie took a quick mental recall of the uniforms who were at the Foulford the night before and didn't recognise him. This meant he could play dumb.

"Morning, sir," The police officer responded.

"Bit of bother?"

"Nothing to concern you, sir. Just cleaning up after a minor incident."

Guthrie noted the man's attempt to downplay what was happening behind him, but any TV junkie who watched any number of cop shows would be able to deduce that a 'minor incident' did not require the presence of people in white suits apparently going over the ground surrounding a parked car in minute detail.

Guthrie pressed the officer. "Oh, aye? Seems like an awful lot of people milling around for nothing, eh?"

The officer tensed and sensed Guthrie's unwillingness to accept the answer he had given.

"Sir, if you don't mind. This is a police matter and in any incident there are routine procedures to follow."

Guthrie took one last look over the fluorescent-clad shoulder of the scene's guardian. Without saying anything, he pushed off and cycled slowly down the road.

Another mile further east and he stopped at the next junction leading off the main road and heading up the hill to his left. Guthrie unclipped his iPhone from the bracket on the handlebar and sat on the grass.

"Bugger!" The grass was still wet from the rain. Standing, he brushed his rear end and backed up to a stone wall. Perching himself on it, he swiped the iPhone into life. He used an app to track his bike rides, but he wanted to open up the map application.

After zooming in on his location, he moved the map around on the screen trying to find out if this second road up the hill was connected to the one Chamber's van was on. There was no easy loop, but it did eventually connect after four miles or so. He plotted out the route and transferred it to his cycling app. All he had to do now was get back on the bike and head up the hill.

Up the hill.

What did they say in the mountain bike world if you wanted to experience the fun downhills? *If you want to ride the prime, you have to do the climb.*

He swung his leg over the bike and started his slow climb.

SEVEN

DECISION

The climb was short but steep. Guthrie had selected first gear on the bike and by the time he reached the crest of the hill he was blowing hard. The air was sharp and every breath was burning his lungs. His legs were shaking, the sweat dripping off his nose. He felt he could wring out his eyebrows.

"Jeez," he said out loud as he dismounted, laid the bike down on the grass verge and grabbed his knees. He gasped for air even though the act of breathing in hurt so much. Standing upright, he unbuckled his helmet and perched it on the handlebar. He turned, hands on his head, to look back down the hill. Deceptively short from the bottom, it had proven to be steep enough that he could have walked to the top faster and expended less energy.

"You have got to get fit," he muttered to himself. He pulled the water bottle from its holder on the bike frame and took a long, cold drink. His heart still raced, and his legs were jelly, so he walked around in circles from one side of the one-lane road to the other. On each rotation he could see the vehicles parked down on the main road. The white

Transit van and the police car standing out in the midst of the various shades of greens and browns of the fields and hedgerows. On the next rotation, he looked further back along the road to the Foulford Inn. Just like the police vehicles, the white of its walls made it easy to spot.

He kept walking from one side of the road to the other. Chambers had been attacked *there*... and walked to *there*... and whoever did it... left going *that* way... or *that* way... or *that* way. He stopped and surveyed the small valley.

There were only three ways to leave the scene. Either direction along the main road, or up the hill on which Chambers had parked. He walked over to the bike and unclipped the phone. He looked again at the map. In that four-mile loop, three other roads branched off and either headed, eventually, back to Crieff to the west or Perth to the east.

Guthrie put the phone in his jacket pocket, picked up the water bottle, and walked along the road towards the far side of the hill. The countryside was typical of this part of Scotland. Not mountainous like the west coast, not rolling farmland like Angus on the east coast, but somewhere in between. Hilly enough to hide narrow roads. Not populated enough for there to be constant traffic. Few houses with hundreds of acres between them.

And on a night like last night, no-one was out and about —except Alexander Chambers and at least one other person.

Guthrie turned back to his bike. What did he think he could find out by cycling around here? *Face it, Guthrie. You're not in the game anymore.*

To his right, there was a gate built into the dry-stone wall. Beyond was another wall running perpendicular and heading back the length of the ridge towards the other road.

A path ran alongside the wall. Guthrie looked to his left and saw a similar arrangement heading off in the opposite direction. A right-of-way. A walker's pathway through this part of the glen. He could see why it would be here versus where the main road snaked its way lazily through the valley. The view was so much better. A walker would be afforded views of several miles in either direction.

Guthrie's legs were feeling better, and his breathing had returned to normal, although his heart rate was still well above watching-TV-on-the-couch level. He picked up his bike, slid the water bottle back into its holder, and plopped his helmet on his head without bothering to clip the strap under his chin. He straddled the bike and exhaled.

He should just call it quits. What was he trying to achieve? What could he achieve? His days of investigating murders and muggings were over.

He had a decision to make. He had to force himself to come to grips with his retirement. Retirement. That was a laugh. Forced to retire. Bloody pencil-pushers. What did they know about real police work?

"Ach." He clipped his helmet strap under his chin and surveyed the road in front of him. Four miles before he could circle back to the other road. Then they'd probably tell him he couldn't continue through because it was a crime scene and he'd have to head back up the hill and either find another way back to the Foulford or double back to where he was right now.

He looked behind him to the hill he just climbed. That would certainly be the easy way back. He wouldn't have to do any work, just freewheel all the way to the flat of the main road. Back to the hotel, a shower, pack up, give his statement, and go home.

"No-brainer."

He spun the pedals so he could push off and stood up on them as he made the tight circle on the road to head back down the hill. As he completed the 180-degree turn next to the grass on the downhill side of the road, something caught his eye.

EIGHT

DOWNHILL

At first, he didn't know what he was looking at. It was mostly brown and merged into the background, but it was a little fleck of white that made him stop and look again. It was propped up against the wall next to the gate. He slowly got off the bike and gently laid it down on the grass next to the road, not taking his eyes off the object. He knelt down and took a closer look. A cloth cap. The various shades of brown camouflaged it against the wall. It had been the small, white label fluttering ever so slightly in the breeze that had caught his eye. It looked brand new so it couldn't have been lying around too long, except Guthrie assumed it was soaked from being out in the rain.

As he was about to stand up, he noticed something on the other side of the gate. He could see the edge of a metal object lying in the grass. He stood up and took a couple of steps to his right. Leaning on the wall, he looked over. It was black and shiny, but he couldn't tell what it was.

His heart started to race. He already knew what this could mean. He clambered over the wall rather than go through the gate. Carefully, he moved the grass away from the object.

"Okay, Guthrie." He slowly stood and backed up, careful not to disturb anything more than he already had. Once back across the wall, he grabbed the bike and jumped on it like he was twenty years younger. As he headed downhill, his heart rate and breathing quickened, this time not because he was pedalling hard. On the contrary, he had to pull on the brake levers to keep his speed in check. The crisp morning air rushed at him. His eyes started to stream.

Approaching the junction with the main road, he looked both ways. Seeing no vehicles, he swung straight out across the road, turning right and heading back towards the police cordon.

He was pedalling now, though.

NINE

OLD HABITS

The back wheel locked up as Guthrie hauled on the brake lever and the bike skidded to a stop at the taped-off junction. The uniformed officer was sitting sideways on the front passenger's seat, legs outside of the marked car. When he saw Guthrie slide to a stop it was everything he could do to get out of the car.

"Hello again, sir," he called to Guthrie.

"Who's in charge here?" Guthrie had set his bike against a fence post which was also anchoring one end of the police tape stretched across the road.

"I'm sorry, sir. Why do you want to know that?"

Guthrie could see it coming. He had sized up the officer during their first encounter and immediately took a disliking to him. He had acted bored and would rather have been anywhere but in the middle of nowhere. He was, apparently, made for bigger and better things than standing guard duty on the corner of a field. He was in his early 30s. Guthrie figured he knew why he was sent out here. He'd seen it before. He was the kind of person nobody wanted to be around, and when this assignment came up, it was the perfect excuse to get him out of the way.

Guthrie took a deep breath, trying to steady his heartbeat. He repeated the question.

"Who's in charge of the scene, constable?" He kept his eyes locked on the officer.

The officer flinched first.

"Just a minute." He turned and walked towards Chamber's vehicle where two white-clad figures were leaning in through the open front doors. The officer stopped well short, not wanting to get his size twelve police-issue boot prints all over the scene. Calling towards the van, one of the white suits looked up. The officer motioned for him to come over. After a short, hushed conversation, in which Guthrie knew the uniform was probably telling the white suit about the rather rude civilian on the bike, the man nodded to the constable and walked towards Guthrie.

"How can I help you, sir?"

"Are you in charge of the scene?" Guthrie asked, still a little out of breath.

The man seemed to take offence at the question as if it wouldn't be evident to anyone that he was the boss. "I am. Detective Inspector Redman."

The man made no attempt to put out a hand but instead folded his arms. Guthrie picked up on the body language and decided to take the high road.

"Look, I'm sorry to take you away from your work, but I think I have some information you might be interested in."

Redman's eyes narrowed. "Oh, aye? What kind of information is that then, sir?"

"I was at the Foulford Inn last night when Mr Chambers died."

"What's your name?"

"Guthrie."

"Okay, Mr Guthrie. I was going to pay you a visit later this morning. What's so important that you had to hop on your bike and come to us?"

"First of all, you need to know I'm a retired DS."

"All right. Didn't know that."

"My fault, I'm afraid. I didn't tell the officers last night. Figured it didn't matter."

"Probably correct, but go on." Redman's pose hadn't changed. He stood with arms folded, eyes narrowed.

"Well, I decided to get up and take a quick bike ride this morning."

"You decided to get up and snoop around and see what you could see, Mr Ex-detective. Am I right?"

Guthrie felt a little put out that Redman had so quickly seen right through him. He didn't respond immediately, but in the few seconds Guthrie took to think of a comeback, Redman raised an eyebrow, and the edge of his mouth turned up in the slightest of half-smiles.

"Bugger!"

"I thought so," Redman said. "So? What do you have for me?"

"Back along the road," Guthrie pointed a thumb over his right shoulder. "There's another road that goes up the hill."

"The Fendoch road. I know it," Redman added.

"After riding past and talking to PC Personality there," the remark drawing a snort from Redman, "I thought I would ride up the hill and take a look at the big picture. I wanted to see where Chambers had walked from and where his assailant could have come or gone."

Redman said nothing, so Guthrie continued.

"To be honest, I was about to head back down the hill

and call it a day. I really didn't know what I thought I could accomplish."

"Just can't stop being a copper, right?"

"Aye, I guess." Guthrie looked over at the constable and the crime scene officers doing their thing. Redman was so right. He wanted more than anything to be on the other side of the plastic tape barrier.

"I found a couple of items you need to look at." Redman, again, said nothing. "Along the ridge, there's a path. Some kind of walking trail or right-of-way or something, you know. On either side of the road there are gates. That's where I stopped. Just before I started back down the hill, I found a cloth cap."

"A cloth cap? What, like a flat cap? A bunnet?"

"Yup. Looks almost brand new. I mean, it doesn't look like it's been out in the elements for a long time."

"Could have been dropped by a hillwalker," Redman countered.

"I did think of that, but then I thought, who wears those things? I didn't think it was a hillwalker. Now, a gamekeeper, perhaps?"

"Mr Guthrie. I think that may be a stretch. You knew Mr Chambers was a gillie, correct?" Guthrie nodded, about to respond, but Redman kept going. "Not every gamekeeper or country estate worker dresses like something out of *Take the High Road*, you know."

"I also found a torch." Guthrie shouted, annoyed at the DI's tone. The uniformed constable looked towards them. Guthrie held up a hand and continued in a normal voice. "I found a torch. A large one. Metal. One that takes probably three D cell batteries."

"Still not convinced," Redman said.

"Ach. C'mon!"

The constable started walking towards the two men. Guthrie looked towards him. Redman saw Guthrie's attention move and turned to face the officer. "It's okay." He turned back to Guthrie.

"You're obviously upsetting PC Williams, and my patience is wearing thin. So you'd better get to the point and convince me that what you have to say is worth the time I'm not spending back here at my crime scene."

"It's not the crime scene."

"Really?" The apparent sarcasm was not lost on Guthrie.

"Chambers was struck on the head. It was quite a blow. I should know, I went through enough towels soaking up his blood last night. The torch I found had a broken lens, and there looked to be a bloodstain on the reflector and the remnants of the lens and bulb."

"Okay. Let's just say I buy the theory. Are you trying to tell me that after the rain we had last night there was still what may or may not have been blood on the torch?"

Guthrie paused. Was he just adding up things that shouldn't be put together? No. He knew he was on to something, but he just didn't have it all neatly packaged in his head.

"Well?"

Guthrie could see Redman was losing his patience. He had to give him a good enough reason to at least check his claim. He racked his brain. What was it? Why was he so sure they were looking in the wrong place?

Suddenly it dawned on him. "The cap!"

"The cap?"

"Yes, the cap. Let's just assume it belongs to Chambers. If he lost it here, if he was attacked here, then how did it end up a mile away at the side of the other road?"

"It blew over there. You did notice it was a little windy last night?"

"Funny. Were you here last night?"

Redman shook his head.

"I was. I wasn't paying attention to the weather, other than I knew there was some and it was happening outside."

Redman let loose a short chuckle despite himself.

"But then when Chambers came into the bar, the rain was blown in the doorway. The floor just inside the door was wet from the rain. The wind was also blowing in. The door from the bar to the car park is on the east end of the building. This means the wind was blowing down the glen from the east."

"And...?"

"And the cap had been blown against the west side of the wall. How could it be blown all the way *up* the hill—against the wind—jump over one wall, cross the road and end up flat against the side of the wall on the other side of the road?"

"It's a magic bunnet?"

"Bloody hell!"

"Okay, okay. Continue."

"I think Chambers was attacked there, for whatever reason. The torch was used as the weapon and then tossed over the wall. Chambers then got into the van and tried to drive down here knowing this was the closest place he could get help."

"Doesn't explain the flat tyre. If he had a flat tyre would he have driven his van down the hill?"

"I think he probably would have. Here's the thing. If you were out in that weather last night, would you have stopped on top of a hill when there was the Foulford not two miles down the road?"

"Perhaps."

"What's the state of the tyre? Front left wasn't it?"

Redman folded his arms. "Very observant, Mr. Guthrie. Yes, front left, and it was in pretty good shape. Just flat."

"Okay. How many people keep driving when they have a puncture? Not many. They mostly stop pretty quickly, right. I think the puncture just happened."

"Just happened?"

"Yes. I think he was attacked on the hill, was driving to the Foulford, got a puncture and walked from where he parked the van."

"You're saying he stopped and walked, rather than keep driving what he knew was a short distance to get to the Foulford?"

"I'm saying he wasn't thinking straight. Would I have kept driving? Probably. But he had been whacked on the head with a large metal object."

"You're asking me to accept one or two assumptions, Mr. Guthrie."

Guthrie looked up. Several small clouds moved slowly across the pale blue sky. When he looked back at Redman, he was resigned to the fact that his head was probably somewhere in the clouds too. Redman stared at him for what seemed like an age but was only a few seconds. He then turned and called over to PC Williams.

"Williams. I need you to give me a ride around the corner."

RIGHT OR WRONG?

By the time Guthrie had showered and changed, DI Redman was waiting for him in the bar of the Foulford. He was nursing a small glass of Coke and looked more like a normal person, far more relaxed now that he was out of his protective white suit. As Guthrie stepped into the bar, he looked up.

"Can I buy you a drink, Mr Guthrie?"

Jim Lawson pulled a pint glass from behind the bar in anticipation.

"Why not. But just an orange juice, eh, Jim." Lawson grabbed a bottle from a small fridge and, after shaking it, popped the cap and poured it into a tall glass. "Cheers," he said as it was handed to him. He sat on a barstool next to Redman. "I figure you still need to officially talk to me about last night."

"Aye, I do."

"But what about the cap and torch?"

Redman took a long sip of his Coke. Placing the glass carefully on a coaster on the bar, he slowly turned his attention back to Guthrie, who rolled his eyes and looked away.

"Sorry," said Redman. "I know you're dying to find out what I think now that I've been up there. It's written all over you."

"I'm that transparent?"

"No. I would be the same way. I see in you what I see in myself."

"So?"

Redman took another slow drink.

"You're a bugger!"

"I'm so transparent?"

"No. I just see in you what I see in myself."

"Ha!" Redman's face broke out in a wide grin. "All right, all right. From what I could see, I think you might be right. I told Williams to look after the current scene and told the SOCO boys to take a look at the top of the hill."

Guthrie smiled. He knew he had something, but from the time he had left Redman at the junction along the glen he had a niggling feeling that he was perhaps just making things produce a picture he wanted to appear.

"I thought I was trying too hard to make it fit."

"Well, you've saved us some time, Mr Guthrie. If you hadn't been such a nosy bugger, we'd still be trudging around in the wrong field."

"You think SOCO will be able to lift any prints?" Guthrie asked.

"I'm not sure. Last night's rain will make it difficult."

Guthrie nodded.

"We do, however, need to sit down and take a formal statement. You obviously know the drill, but if your theory is right, you were all over that scene on your bike. I know you were here last night, but let's get it all down on paper before we let anything slip through the cracks."

ELEVEN

GOODBYES

After Guthrie had given his statement to Redman, he put his suitcase in the car and secured his bike to the carrier. He wanted to make sure he said his goodbyes. Jen completed his check-out. He hugged her and asked where her father was.

"Try out in the garage. He's probably tinkering on something out there."

Guthrie thanked her again, made his way through the bar and out the door that Chambers had burst through less than twenty-four hours previously. A small outbuilding served as Jim Lawson's garage. On one side there was a car covered by a large, grey sheet. On the other side, an old Land Rover. Lawson's legs were sticking out from underneath.

"Jim," Guthrie called. "It's me, Tom. I just wanted to say cheerio."

Lawson scooted himself out from under the old Landy. Standing up, he wiped his hands on an oil-stained cloth. "Sorry," he said, indicating the state of his overalls and dirty skin. "Wasn't expecting to be seen in public for a while."

Guthrie smiled. "It's no bother, Jim." He put out his hand and Lawson shook it. "I'm sorry about last night. I know it was a shock for you and Jen. If there's anything I can do, please call me. I gave Jen my mobile number."

"That's very kind."

Lawson looked at his feet. He began rubbing his hands with the oily rag again. The silence was awkward. Guthrie looked around the garage.

"So this is where you get away from all us punters, eh?"

"Aye. What do they call these things? It's my man cave."

Guthrie laughed. "What's under here?" he pointed to the mystery car.

"Och, just a project I've been working on for a while. Roadworthy, but not quite finished. I'll probably sell it now I have the Land Rover. Better suited for the winters through here." Lawson grabbed a corner of the sheet and rolled it back, revealing an MGB GT.

"Jeez, I love these cars," Guthrie said.

For the next half hour, Guthrie and Lawson chatted about the cars they had owned through the years and ones they wished they had but never did. When they finally parted, Guthrie repeated his offer for Lawson to call him any time. He also said that he wanted to come back before the winter set in to see if he could try the biking thing again.

"Let's just hope it's a little more peaceful than this weekend. In more ways than one."

Guthrie agreed. They shook hands again and Guthrie walked out of the garage. Getting in the car, he pulled out into the road and headed towards Perth, taking him back past PC Personality. A mile later, he passed the second junction. This time it was blocked just like the other. He watched it grow smaller in the rearview mirror until it disappeared as the road curved. He sighed loudly.

TWELVE

REFRESHED

Guthrie unfastened the straps securing his mountain bike to the carrier, lifted it off and wheeled it over to a small, stone shed behind his flat that served as a utility building. Inside were various tools used by the landlord to keep the grass mown, borders trimmed, and the building in good condition. He found a hose neatly coiled around a plastic holder on wheels. After dragging it out to the courtyard, he connected one end to a spigot and unwound the hose. His bike was leaning up against the moss-covered wall that separated the courtyard from the adjoining property.

Pointing the hose at the bike, he pressed the trigger and let the spray of water release and wash away the dirt from the wheels.

It felt good to get back in the saddle, he thought to himself. He waved the spray of water back and forth over the bike.

Back in the saddle. There's a thought.

He turned the bike around, quickly washing the other side. After drying it off, he put it away in his storage locker.

Upstairs in his flat, he put the kettle on for a coffee.

Taking a seat at a small desk, situated against one wall of his living room, he fired up his computer. He opened a web browser and, pulling up a search engine, tapped on the keyboard:

private investigter licence scotland

After a couple of seconds, the screen refreshed and the search engine was asking him a question.

*Did you mean: private **investigator** licence **Scotland**?*

Guthrie read the question and said, "Bugger. Aye."

He found a small notebook in his desk drawer and started clicking on the search results.

NOTES ON WRUNG OUT

The places described in WRUNG OUT are a mix of real and fictional.

Tayside Police Headquarters were indeed housed at West Bell Street and the building is now the home of Police Scotland for this part of the country.

Guthrie's flat is based on a real building in Broughty Ferry, which sticks out because of its modern design, sitting among the more traditional Victorian buildings on the same street.

Guthrie's methods and those of the officers of Tayside Police are entirely fictional in nature. I apologise to all the Bobbies who may read this and say, "That's not how we do things," or "They'd never get away with that."

WRUNG OUT was originally an exercise in creating, for my own personal use, a backstory for Tom Guthrie. In publishing it, I am aware that there are probably errors in language, punctuation and the rest. It comes to you raw—a translation of the pictures in my mind to words on a page.

I know I came away with a different take on Mr Guthrie from one with which I started a few months before I began the process of writing the first full-length Tom Guthrie novel, TOOLS OF THE TRADE.

I hope you liked it and will pardon my indulgence.

— Allan L Mann

Georgetown, KY, January 2015

NOTES ON MURDER IN THE SMA' GLEN

Since MURDER IN THE SMA' GLEN is based on real events, I walked a fine line between changing all the names completely, and wishing to pay my respects, in a very small way, to people who were touched by what was a terrible experience for those close to a murder.

The facts are far more bizarre than what I invented for this short story.

The places described in the story, therefore, are a mix of real and fictional.

The Foulford Inn is located on the A822 just east of Crieff, Perthshire. There has been an inn located there since 1785, but in 2010 it transitioned to a holiday cottage. It is still owned and run by the same family who were caught up in the real life drama, upon which MURDER IN THE SMA' GLEN is based, back in 1926.

The layout of the countryside around the Foulford would be somewhat recognisable, but the roads have been created to suit the story.

Guthrie's methods and those of the police officers are

entirely fictional in nature. I apologise to all the Bobbies and other professionals who may read this and cringe.

WRUNG OUT, the first Tom Guthrie short story, began as an exercise in creating, for my own personal use, a backstory for Tom Guthrie while working on TOOLS OF THE TRADE. At the same time, I came across the real mystery of Alexander Chalmers. It seemed too good to pass up.

I hope you enjoyed learning more about Tom Guthrie. Thank you for spending some time with him.

— Allan L Mann

Georgetown, KY, February 2015

THE REAL SMA' GLEN MYSTERY

Back in 1926, Alexander Chalmers died. The circumstances surrounding how he died were somewhat confused and no-one was charged with causing his death. Rather, an inquiry found that it had been an accident.

I came across the story in an article published in *The Courier*. This story sent me down the path resulting in MURDER IN THE SMA' GLEN.

JOHN GORRIE, proprietor of the Foulford Inn and Hotel, and his daughter, Betty, help Alexander Chalmers, a 65 year-old delivery driver into the inn after finding him sitting in his horse-drawn van, face covered in blood.

"I have been struck on the head. They hit me with a lamp," Chalmers told Betty, once he had been helped inside the inn and placed on the floor. While Betty was tending to his wounds, Chalmers died.

Chalmers had started out on the morning of October 9th, 1926, driving his delivery van for D&J McEwan, merchants. As the day progressed, the storm, one of the worst in years, became more and more severe. He continued to make deliveries to farms in the area.

Robert Stirton, a 21 year-old motorvan driver, arrived at the inn and said that he had seen a lamp lying on the road. This road, however, was not one Chalmers would have normally travelled.

Police Inspector John Robertson and Dr. Haig examined Chalmers' body and concluded that the injuries would not in themselves been enough to kill Chalmers, but the combination of shock and the cold weather would have been enough to do him in.

Stirton also indicated that he saw a small motorcar close to where Chalmers may have been attacked.

Deputy Chief Constable MacPherson joined the inquiry team. They interviewed William Ridley who lived a mile from the Foulford Inn. Ridley had passed Chalmers' van on the night he died and seen him crouched up against the wind. Ridley apparently called to Chalmers, but he did not answer.

The next day, Ridley's sister found Chalmers' blood-covered hat in a field.

Three months after the death, Sheriff Valentine and a jury consisting of two women and five men recorded an unanimous verdict of accidental death.

At the time, *The Courier* ran an editorial stating:

"...that until outstanding questions were answered the Sma' Glen mystery could never be considered solved."

BUT THE STORY doesn't end there.

According to an article published in the *Police Gazette*,

a local woman who had "the second sight" said that the murderer was physically deformed and would meet a violent death.

A rabbit trapper with a club foot, who was vying for the attention of the same woman in whom Alexander Chalmers was interested, was on his bicycle heading down the very steep King Street in Crieff, when he came off his bike and fell into the path of a road-roller. He survived the accident but was severely injured. Before he died the police interviewed him hoping for a deathbed confession.

He admitted nothing.

SO THE TRUTH behind the death of Alexander Chalmers remains a mystery.

ACKNOWLEDGMENTS

My thanks go out to many people, but there are always those who deserve particular mention.

Thank you to both *The Courier* and Chris Ferguson, Assistant Editor, who brought the story of Alexander Chalmers to light again in that excellent local newspaper.

Brian and Maureen Beaumont run Foulford South Wing, the current incarnation of the Foulford Inn. There is indeed a 9-hole golf course on the property, and you can spend a wonderful, relaxing time in the Perthshire countryside with Brian and Maureen as your hosts. Maureen provided me with information about the death of Alexander Chalmers, including the story of what happened to the prime suspect in the case.

A big thank you to my wife, Christy, who helps to proof-read, and provides feedback and encouragement. I can't do what I do without both (and the many cups of tea and chocolate biscuits).

ABOUT THE AUTHOR

Allan lives in Georgetown, Kentucky. He and his wife, Christy, have three daughters, Katie, Emily, and Maureen. Allan grew up on the East coast of Scotland, and has been a professional pilot his entire career. He thought writing books would be much simpler. He was wrong.

The two short stories that make up WHEN IT RAINS are prequels to *The Angus Murder Mysteries* series set in the area Allan knows best —Angus.

ALSO BY ALLAN L MANN

A CURRENT LISTING OF ALL BOOKS CAN ALWAYS
BE FOUND AT WWW.ALLANLMANN.COM

Tools of the Trade

Wind Damage